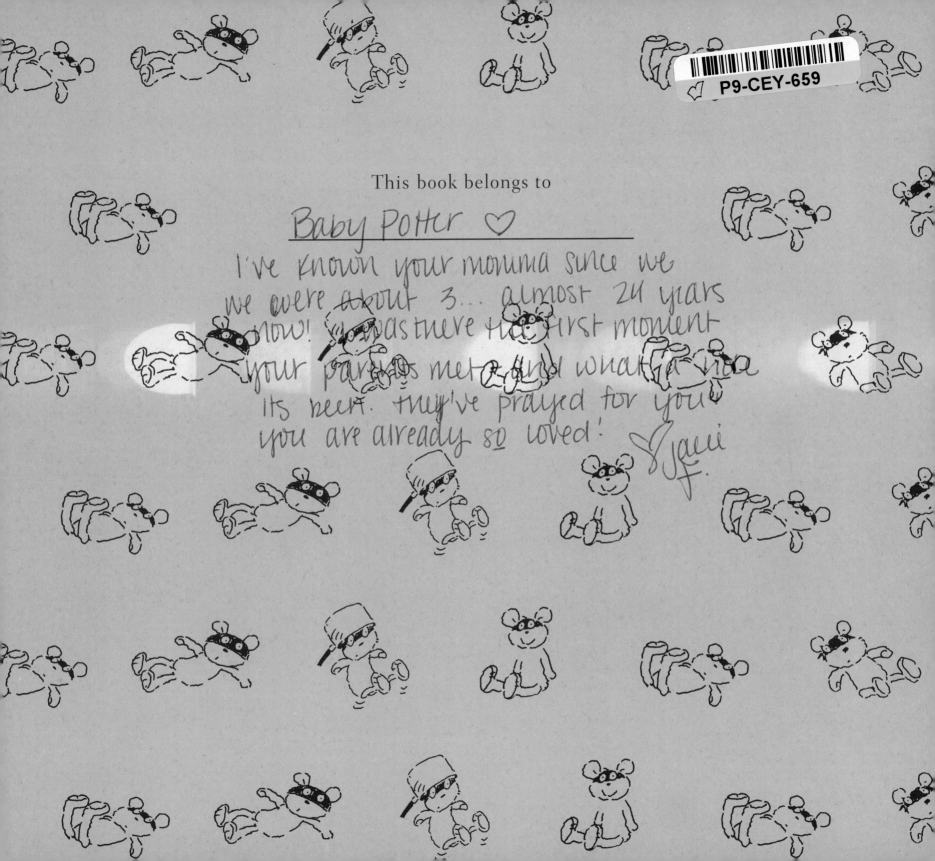

This book belongs to

Baby Potter ♡

I've known your momma since we
we were ~~about~~ 3... almost 24 years
now! I was there the first moment
your parents met and what a ride
its been. they've prayed for you!
you are already so loved!
♡ Jani F.

Do Super Heroes Have Teddy Bears?

By Carmela LaVigna Coyle Illustrated by Mike Gordon

Color by Molly Hahn

TAYLOR TRADE PUBLISHING

Lanham · New York · Boulder · Toronto · Plymouth, UK

Published by Taylor Trade Publishing
An imprint of The Rowman & Littlefield Publishing Group, Inc.
4501 Forbes Boulevard, Suite 200, Lanham, Maryland 20706
www.rowman.com

Estover Road, Plymouth PL6 7PY, United Kingdom

Distributed by National Book Network

British Library Cataloguing in Publication Information Available

Library of Congress Cataloging-in-Publication Data Available
978-1-58979-693-5 (cloth)
978-1-58979-694-2 (electronic)

Printed in China
Shenzhen, Guangdong, China
Date of Production: September 2012

To my son Nicky . . . and all your superness!
— c l v c

Do super heroes make capes with blankies and string?

We can turn blankies into
most anything.

Do super heroes take teddies along for the ride?

That's something super heroes get to decide.

Are heroes always brave and daring?

We're brave and bold and kind and caring.

Do they get bored when there's nothing to do?

That's when we decide to invent something new!

Can they make spaceships out of boxes and tape?

Especially whenever we have to escape!

Do heroes ever come home
muddy and wet?

You'll be amazed at how
messy we'll get.

Do super heroes have to fix what they break?

Even when it was a silly mistake?

Does a super hero hide where no one will look?

Here's a top-secret cubby to read our new book.

Do heroes always eat their carrots and peas?

Open your mouth for the airplane, please!

Does a super hero have to help with the dishes?

Unless there's a genie who'll grant us some wishes.

Is there still enough time
to save the day?

*I'm sure you will in your
very own way.*

Are super heroes ticklish from head to toe?

I guess there's really just one way to know.

Do they get scared when
you turn off the light?

Not after a hug and
a kiss nighty-night.

Are super heroes and heroes exactly the same?

Maybe the difference is all in the name . . .

Be your own *hero!*

Draw your own **HERO** here!

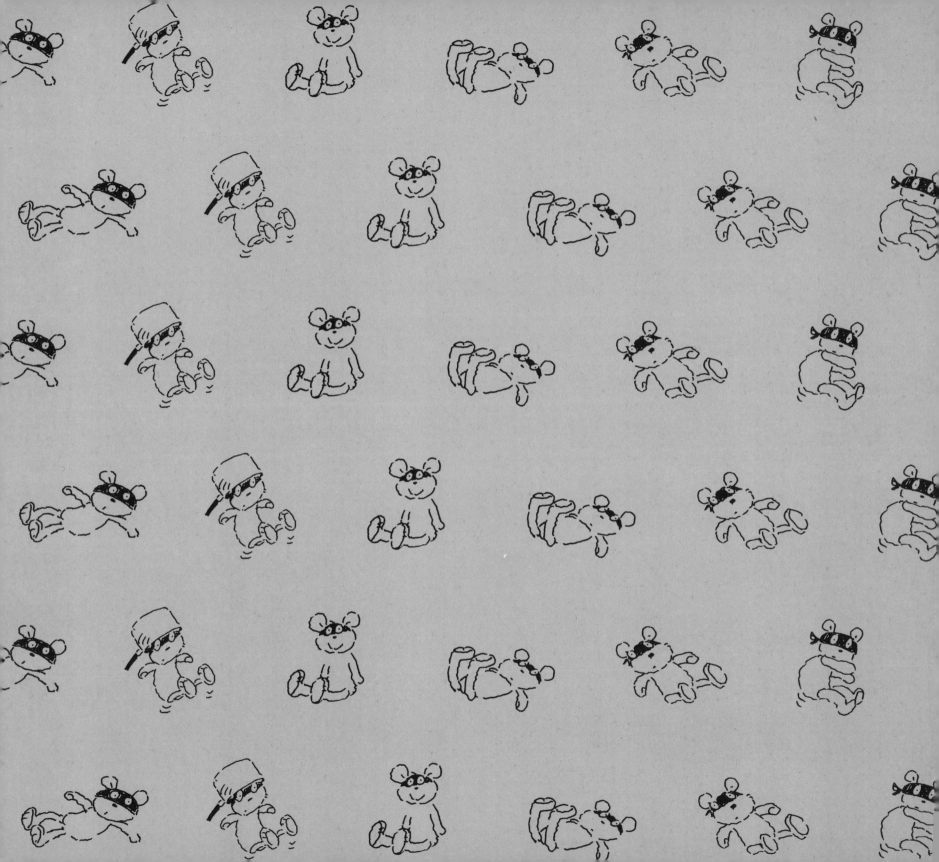